Unicorn Academy
...Where magic happens!

Zara and Moonbeam

JULIE
SYKES

illustrated by
LUCY
TRUMAN

nosy
crow

For Khadijah and her magical mum, Rumena Aktar

First published in the UK in 2020 by Nosy Crow Ltd
The Crow's Nest, 14 Baden Place
Crosby Row, London, SE1 1YW

www.nosycrow.com

ISBN: 978 1 78800 927 0

Nosy Crow and associated logos are trademarks
and/or registered trademarks of Nosy Crow Ltd.

Text copyright © Julie Sykes and Linda Chapman, 2020
Illustrations copyright © Lucy Truman, 2020
Cover typography © Joel Holland, 2020

A CIP catalogue record for this book is available from the British Library.

Printed and bound in Great Britain by Clays Ltd, Elcograf S.p.A.

Papers used by Nosy Crow are made from
wood grown in sustainable forests.

MIX
Paper from
responsible sources
FSC® C018072

1 3 5 7 9 10 8 6 4 2

CHAPTER ONE

"We won!" Zara punched the air as her unicorn, Moonbeam, galloped across the dry grass and plunged into Sparkle Lake.

"Yay!" Moonbeam kicked up her hooves, showering them both with the glittering water.

Zara pushed her straight brown hair away from her face. "Hurry up, slowcoaches!" she called to her friends. "It's lovely and cool!"

With whoops of delight, Phoebe, Lily and Aisha galloped into the lake on their unicorns Shimmer, Feather and Silver.

"It was so hot and stuffy this morning in class,

I honestly thought I was going to die. I think we should ask Ms Rosemary if we can have afternoon lessons in the lake," said Phoebe, pushing her long blonde plaits over her shoulders. "It would be awesome!"

Zara laughed. "Yep, cos she'll *definitely* agree to that!"

It was the middle of the summer and Unicorn Island was suffering from a heatwave. At first, Zara and her friends in Amethyst dormitory had loved the long hot days and nights. But after several weeks of soaring temperatures the heat was becoming unbearable. The grass had dried to a yellow crisp and the flowers and plants had all wilted. The fountain was reduced to half its height and the lake had shrunk, leaving a rim of cracked dried mud around the edge.

The unicorns splashed around, kicking water at each other with their hooves.

Zara and Moonbeam

Lily leaned forward and whispered in Feather's ear. Suddenly the lake began to ripple. Zara smelled the sweet sugary scent of magic and saw sparkles bubbling up through the water from Feather's hooves. The ripples grew stronger until the water rose in a tall, glittering wave. It arched high over Zara, Phoebe and Aisha. Zara held her breath, expecting a soaking.

CRACK! More magical sparkles fizzed in the air and the wave exploded, raining shimmering droplets down on everyone.

Zara laughed, enjoying the cool mist falling on her face and hair.

Lily, Phoebe and Aisha clapped and cheered. "Go, Feather and Shimmer!"

Zara clapped too but she couldn't help feeling a little bit envious. She knew Lily's unicorn, Feather, had created the wave with her special moving magic and Phoebe's unicorn, Shimmer,

3

had broken it with his energy magic. When would Moonbeam discover her magic? The unicorns usually found their special magical powers during their first year at the academy. Those who didn't had to stay on for a second year with their partners.

"He's coming back," Moonbeam whispered.

Zara leaned over her neck. "Who's coming back?" she asked, wondering what Moonbeam was talking about.

"He is," said Moonbeam dreamily.

"But who?" said Zara. "Who are you talking about?" She felt a prickle of frustration. Moonbeam often went off into daydreams. "What do you mean, Moonbeam?"

Moonbeam started in surprise as if she was waking up. "Oh, sorry! I'm not sure what I was saying."

"Hurry up, you two!" Lily called from the bank. "Lunchtime's nearly over and we need to dry off

before afternoon classes start."

"OK," Zara called. "We're coming!"

But Moonbeam didn't move. "Zara, wait, I feel strange, like there's magic all around me. My skin's tingling."

Zara shrugged. "Shimmer and Feather were just doing magic. That must be what you can sense."

"This is different," Moonbeam insisted. "For a moment back there I … I felt like I'd found my own magic."

Zara frowned. "But you didn't do anything magical, Moonbeam."

"No, but I had a feeling," said Moonbeam.

Zara sighed. Moonbeam was always going on about feelings and how important they were. "Moonbeam, you know I want you to find your magic just as much as you do but imagining it's happening isn't going to help. Come on, let's go

and dry off. We've got Care of Unicorns after lunch and Ms Rosemary hates it when people are late."

For a moment, she thought Moonbeam was going to argue but then, to her relief, she splashed out of the lake. As they reached the bank, Zara slid from Moonbeam's back and ran over to join her friends, who were sunbathing.

"That was a fun water fight!" she said, flopping down on the grass next to Phoebe.

Aisha giggled and tightened her high ponytail. "I thought Feather was going to cover us with that wave!"

Phoebe grinned. "It wasn't half as scary as the enormous tidal wave that almost hit us when we camped on the cliff though."

Lily nodded. "I will never ever forget that. It was terrifying! We were so lucky that Shimmer was able to save us using his energy magic."

Back in the spring, a huge tidal wave had nearly destroyed a stretch of coastline that the girls had been camping on. They'd only escaped thanks to Shimmer's magic powers. He had used his ability to throw balls of magic energy to break up the wave before it could do any real damage.

That wasn't the only environmental disaster the girls had experienced this year. Just after they had started at Unicorn Academy, purple tornadoes had devastated the island. One had almost destroyed the academy, but Feather had used her moving magic to force it safely out to sea.

Zara suddenly had a worrying thought. "What if this heatwave is being caused by the same person who caused the tornadoes and the tidal wave?"

Phoebe sat up. "You mean it could be part of someone's evil plan?"

"It's a possibility," said Zara.

"If it is part of someone's plan, we need to be on our guard," said Lily.

Phoebe waved her hands dramatically. "We could be attacked at any moment!"

"Don't exaggerate, Phoebs," Zara said with a grin. She really liked Phoebe but she did turn every small thing into a huge drama.

"But what if this evil person is planning to use this heatwave to hurt us – and our unicorns?" Phoebe exclaimed.

"We need to find out who's causing these things before it gets worse," said Zara. "We know it's a man because we heard a man's voice in the tornado and tidal wave saying he wouldn't be stopped. And before the tsunami struck, we heard that a cloaked man had been hanging around the outskirts of the village where the wave was heading."

"None of those things tells us who the person is

though," Lily pointed out. "Or why he's trying to harm the island."

"True." A look of determination crossed Zara's eyes. "I vote we try to find him and stop him for good." She glanced round at her three friends. "Who's with me? Who wants to solve this mystery?"

"Me!" cried Phoebe, Lily and Aisha, as their unicorns whinnied and stamped their hooves.

CHAPTER TWO

The girls excitedly discussed ideas for how to track down the evil man as they rode back to the stables at the end of lunchtime.

"Zara," Moonbeam said, as she and Zara reached her stable. "Can I talk to you? It's about these feelings I keep having."

Zara wanted to talk about the mystery but she forced herself to smile. "Of course."

"I might be wrong," said Moonbeam. "But I keep seeing pictures in my head and when I do, I start to say strange stuff out loud. Do you think it could be my magic?"

"Your magic? But, Moonbeam, the stuff you say, well, it's just…" Zara caught herself. She'd been about to say *rubbish*. "It just doesn't seem to mean anything much," she finished.

Moonbeam frowned. "But what if it does mean something? What if it's important?"

Zara stroked her. She really wanted Moonbeam to find her magic but seeing pictures in her head

and saying strange things didn't sound much like magic to her. "I really don't think it has anything to do with your magic powers," she said. "But I'm sure you'll find them soon," she added quickly.

Ms Rosemary was waiting for them in the stables, wearing a big floppy hat and sunglasses.

"Good afternoon," she said when the students had all arrived. "Today we are learning how to keep our unicorns cool. Can anyone think of a way?"

Spike from Topaz dorm put his hand up. "Make them wear sunglasses and a big hat, just like yours, Ms R!"

Everyone burst out laughing and Ms Rosemary smiled. "That's an interesting idea, Spike. I'll think about it," she said. "Any other suggestions?"

A familiar sharp voice cut across her.

"Heatstroke is a serious matter, Ms Rosemary. Rather than making jokes, don't you think you

should be educating the students about what to do in the current weather conditions?"

Zara's heart sank as Mr Longnose, the tall, thin school inspector, strutted through the stable door. Ms Tulip, the riding teacher, was hurrying along behind him. Why was he back? He'd inspected the academy only a few months ago.

"Not him again," groaned Phoebe.

Moonbeam gasped. "Zara!" she hissed. "I was right! I said someone was coming back, didn't I?"

Zara patted her. "It's just a coincidence, Moonbeam. You can't really think you saw into the future that Mr Longnose would come back today. You're letting your imagination run away with you."

Moonbeam hung her head. "Maybe," she muttered.

"I wonder why he's here," whispered Lily. Ms Rosemary was clearly wondering the same thing.

"Good afternoon, Mr Longnose," she said. "What brings you back to the academy so soon? I thought your inspection was complete."

Mr Longnose mopped his forehead with a perfectly ironed hanky. "I inspected the school but I didn't have opportunity to inspect the stables or the quality of riding lessons."

Ms Tulip stepped forward. "As part of the inspector's visit – and so he can experience the teaching first-hand – I have offered to teach him to ride." She tucked a dark curl of hair behind her ear and blushed. "Would you like to come and meet Rocket, my unicorn, Mr Longnose?" she asked.

"Indeed I would," Mr Longnose said.

"Then, please – follow me."

"Urgh!" whispered Phoebe as Ms Tulip led Mr Longnose into the stable block.

"Poor Ms Tulip!" agreed Zara. "I can't think

of anything worse than teaching bossy Mr Longnose."

"Did you see the way she was buttering him up? She must be hoping he gives her a good report." Phoebe fluttered her hands and fluffed up her hair. Imitating Ms Tulip perfectly she simpered, "Oh, let me teach you to ride, Mr Longnose!"

Lily rushed to Ms Tulip's defence. "Don't be mean. Mr Longnose had better give Ms Tulip's teaching a good report or I'll … I'll complain about *him*!"

Aisha nodded in agreement. "I don't see why he's come back. He spent lots of time watching our riding lessons with Ms Tulip when he was here before. Why does he need to see more?"

"I hope he falls off Rocket," grumbled Phoebe. She clapped a hand over her mouth. "Actually, I didn't mean that. I hope he learns to ride super-fast, gives lovely Ms Tulip a brilliant report and

then goes away again really quickly!"

"Me too," said Lily. "It's bad enough having to deal with a heatwave without having to put up with Mr Longnose too!"

Her words sent a thought exploding into Zara's mind. She gasped.

"What? What is it?" demanded Lily.

But before Zara could speak, Ms Rosemary clapped her hands together for silence. "Right. Pay attention, please. This afternoon we are going to make a sun cream to protect your unicorn's nose. The ingredients and equipment are laid out

in the storeroom. Go and collect everything and read through the instructions."

While the rest of the class headed for the storeroom, Zara pulled her friends into a huddle.

"What's going on?" said Phoebe eagerly. "You look like a snot-nosed flapdoodle just sneezed on you!"

"It's Mr Longnose!" hissed Zara. "Maybe he's the person causing all the problems! We know he's very clever and studied geology at university. What if he's responsible for all the extreme weather we've had this year? He was with us when the tidal wave struck and he's here now just when the heatwave is getting really bad." She gazed round at her friends. "Maybe the extreme weather we've had this year has been caused by him!"

CHAPTER THREE

"Girls! What are you doing?" Ms Rosemary's voice cut across the stable yard. "I told you to get your ingredients and instructions. Stop chattering and hurry up!"

"Sorry, miss!" said Zara quickly. "We'll talk about this later," she hissed to the others, as they jogged to the storeroom.

All through the lesson, Zara's mind raced. Could Mr Longnose really be the culprit? The more she thought about it, the more everything seemed to fit together. *But suspicions are not enough*, she reminded herself firmly. *There has to be proof!*

She was so busy thinking about it that she added too much honey powder to her sun cream. She only realised when Moonbeam couldn't stop sneezing after she tried to lick the cream off her nose because it tasted so good!

As soon as the lesson was over, the girls raced up to their dorm where they could talk in private. Amethyst dorm had four beds set around the room, each with a lavender-coloured bedspread. There was a large fluffy purple rug on the floor, which they all sat on in a circle.

"It's him! You're right, Zara. I'm sure of it!" exclaimed Phoebe. "Mr Longnose is so horrible. He's really bossy and a complete show-off!"

"We've got to tell the teachers," said Lily.

"No," said Zara quickly. "At the moment all we have are suspicions and no proof, although the evidence does seem to point to him. Listen." She pulled a mini notebook from her pocket where she had scribbled some notes. "Number one: Mr Longnose is very clever. He's written all sorts of scientific articles. He might know a way to make bad weather happen."

"Or he could be in league with someone who

21

does," said Phoebe excitedly. "He doesn't have a unicorn himself but he may be working with someone who has a unicorn that can do weather magic."

"Good point," said Zara.

"What else have you got on your list?" asked Lily.

"Number two: The first time Mr Longnose arrived at the academy was just as the dormant volcano near the school began to wake up. It was activity from that volcano that caused the tidal wave, so maybe he did something to the volcano on his way here.

"Number three: It was his idea to go camping on the west coast where we were almost drowned by the tidal wave." Zara paused to look round at her friends. "He wanted us to go there!"

Phoebe pretended to be the inspector. "*Volcanoes are a particular interest of mine.*" Her eyes glimmered

with excitement exactly like Mr Longnose's did when he was showing off about how clever he was.

"But why would Mr Longnose want to cause such horrible things to happen to the island?" said Aisha.

"Well," said Zara. "I looked Mr Longnose up when he was here last time and discovered that he was all set for a career in research but he couldn't find anyone to sponsor his work. That's how he ended up as a school inspector. Maybe he wants to get back at the island because no one would fund his research."

Phoebe's eyes widened. "Or ... or..." she spluttered in her excitement, "maybe he thinks that if enough bad weather happens then people will pay for him to do research and he'll be able to stop being an inspector!"

"Great idea, Phoebs!" said Zara excitedly,

writing it down.

"What about the other clues we had – the cloaked stranger with the top hat who was seen by the deserted cottage, and the button we found there," said Lily. "The stranger couldn't have been Mr Longnose. He was at the academy with us when the villagers say they spotted him."

"That's true," said Zara slowly. "I suppose the stranger at the cottage could be completely unrelated to the tidal wave. It could be a red herring – that's what false clues are called."

"What about the button?" asked Aisha.

Zara jumped to her feet and fetched the button from her bedside drawer. "This could be a red herring too,' she said, turning the pale-grey button over in her fingers. It looked expensive and had an ornate engraving on it that looked like a two-headed serpent twisted around a strange symbol.

"Or it could have been dropped by Mr Longnose

at some point when we were there," said Phoebe, as Zara put the button down so they could all see it. "He could have gone to the cottage when we were getting our campsites ready and done something there that caused the tidal wave to hit."

"If you look at the engraving, it almost looks like a letter in really curly writing," said Aisha, tracing the pattern with one finger.

"It's an L!" said Lily with a gasp. "Look everyone! L for Longnose!"

"I knew it!" exclaimed Phoebe triumphantly. "He *is* the evil villain!"

"We don't know for definite that it's his or that he's responsible for these weather disasters," said Zara quickly. "We need to find hard evidence."

"How do we do that?" demanded Phoebe.

Zara grinned. "We spy on him, of course!"

Phoebe squealed in delight. "Oh yes, let's do that! We'll prove he's to blame!"

Zara's eyes shone. "And if he is, we'll stop him, no matter what!"

After dinner that evening there was an interdorm quiz. It was held outside, where it was cooler. Zara, Phoebe, Lily and Aisha carried some blankets out and spread them under an apple tree. When everyone had gathered, Ms Nettles handed out

paper and a pencil to each group.

"Ready?" she asked, smiling round at the assembled students. "Then the first question is, which rare species of beetle lives in the crater of a volcano?"

"The fire beetle," Zara whispered to the others.

Everyone stared at her. "How do you know that?" hissed Phoebe.

Zara grinned. "You know science is my thing. I read up on volcanoes when Mount Inferno suddenly became active again."

The quiz questions covered everything – care of unicorns, geology, famous scientists, wild animals and general knowledge. Zara conferred with her group in whispers before she wrote down each answer. Topaz dorm, who were near to them, were the opposite, talking loudly, especially Spike and Johan, who seemed to be competing to come up with the silliest answer.

"How long are the legs of the very rare, gold-striped, pygmy unicorn?" asked Ms Nettles.

"Long enough to reach the ground!" shouted Spike, earning a fierce glare from Mr Longnose as he arrived late with Ms Tulip.

Mr Longnose had a rug tucked under his arm and Ms Tulip was carrying a jug of iced blackcurrant juice and two glasses on a tray. She spread the rug on the ground near Ms Nettles and then she poured Mr Longnose a drink.

"She really is trying her

hardest to get a good report!" whispered Phoebe.

Ms Nettles waited for them to sit down before continuing. "Who was first person to successfully combine science with magic?"

"Count Lysander Thornberry," Mr Longnose rapped out immediately. "He used science to amplify magic to make a rain machine. I was at university with him. He could have been an amazing research scientist but he took offence when a few academic papers were published questioning whether his weather machines were needed when we have unicorns who can work weather magic. He left the university and became a recluse, returning to his family castle to continue his work there."

Ms Nettles blinked. "Thank you for answering the question so fully, Mr Longnose, but the quiz is for the students."

Mr Longnose raised his eyebrows. "I really

believe you need more challenging questions, Ms Nettles. Perhaps you will allow me to ask a question. What did Count Thornberry call his rain machine?"

"The Big Drip!" hissed Spike in a staged whisper.

Everyone started to giggle but Mr Longnose silenced them with a glare. "The *Pluviam Machina*. Really, Ms Nettles, I am surprised that the pupils here are so lacking in scientific knowledge. Perhaps I should run some classes to teach you about the incredible scientists who've graced our island."

"I would sign up for those!" Ms Tulip said eagerly.

"Ooh, me too!" whispered Phoebe, imitating Ms Tulip's goofy expression.

"Stop it!" giggled Zara. "You'll get us into trouble."

Ms Nettles pursed her lips. "Thank you, Mr Longnose. Now, if I may continue with our quiz?"

The quiz ran over time thanks to Mr Longnose's continued interruptions. Amethyst dorm cheered loudly when Ms Nettles announced them the winners. She handed them a massive bag of sweets. "Don't eat your prize all at once," she said.

Mr Longnose sniffed. "Educational books would have been a more suitable prize." He pulled out his hanky and dabbed at his brow. Even outside, the heat was stifling.

"Right, everyone, one last check on your unicorns and then off to bed!" said Ms Nettles, ignoring him.

Mr Longnose offered his hand to help Ms Tulip up. "Will you accompany me to the stables and talk me through the students' evening routine, Ms Tulip?"

"Of course," she said.

Zara watched them head towards the stables. *Be very careful, Mr Longnose*, she thought. *We're on to you, so you'd better watch out!*

CHAPTER FOUR

The next day, Amethyst dorm used their free time to spy on Mr Longnose. The remote-controlled trolleys that moved bales of straw around the stables were useful for cover. The girls hid behind them and watched him following Ms Tulip around the stable block, clipboard in hand. Then they watched him having a riding lesson in the arena, sitting in front of Ms Tulip on her unicorn, Rocket, as she instructed him.

It was fun spying on Mr Longnose but they didn't see him do anything suspicious. *Not that he would do anything when he's with Ms Tulip*, Zara

thought as she headed back to Amethyst's dorm after supper to fetch a book. *We need to spy on him when he's on his own, maybe sneak into his room...*

Her thoughts were interrupted by the sight of Mr Longnose crossing the corridor ahead of her and climbing a spiral staircase that led up one of the towers. Zara frowned. *Why is he going up there?* There were only two rooms up that staircase – Diamond dormitory on the first floor and a storeroom at the very top.

Intrigued, Zara ran after Mr Longnose. At the half-landing between the two floors, she heard Mr Longnose's footsteps stop. She halted, hovering outside the

door to Diamond dorm. If he came back she'd have to pretend she was just going to see one of the girls there. She listened hard and heard a door open.

Zara waited. What was Mr Longnose doing? She crept on up the stairs to the half-landing where there was a large wooden cupboard in the wall. Zara pushed at the door gently, her heart thudding. What would she do if Mr Longnose was inside? But to her relief, she saw that it was empty apart from a stack of old packing crates and some cardboard boxes.

Zara continued up the top floor but to her astonishment there was no sign of Mr Longnose there either. Where had he gone? She stepped inside the storeroom, picking her way between the students' suitcases, shelves of empty potion bottles and some old paintings to the window. It was covered in dust. Mr Longnose hadn't left by

the window unless he could fly!

Feeling very puzzled, Zara went downstairs. This didn't make sense. Mr Longnose had definitely gone up the stairs. So where was he now? She wanted to talk to the others but the dorm room was empty. Glancing at the clock, she realised it was getting late and her friends must have gone to the stables to settle their unicorns for the night. Zara felt a pang of guilt. Moonbeam would be wondering where she was. She hurried outside, running across the dry grass to the stable block.

Moonbeam whickered happily when she saw her. "There you are!" she said. "I was worried that I'd done something to upset you."

"Of course not!" Zara laid her head against Moonbeam's neck. "I'm sorry I was late. Something really weird happened, Moonbeam… Moonbeam?" She felt a pang of worry as she saw

that Moonbeam's eyelids had closed and she was swaying slightly.

"I see a cloaked man," Moonbeam whispered. "And a dark-green book."

Zara put a hand on her side to steady her. "Are you feeling OK?"

Moonbeam's eyes stayed closed. "A red desert that stretches on and rocks falling from the sky," she intoned. "Danger comes."

Zara frowned. "Moonbeam! What's happening to you? Is it the heat? Do you want a drink?" It was very warm in the stables despite the fans that Ms Tulip had installed when the heatwave showed no sign of breaking.

Moonbeam's eyes flew open. "What just happened?"

"I don't know, you went all weird," said Zara. "You were saying stuff about a cloaked man and a book, a desert and rocks."

"I was seeing pictures in my head again, Zara. Clearer this time." Excitement lit up Moonbeam's dark eyes. "I think I've started to see things that are going to happen. Yesterday, I had a vision about a man arriving at the school and then, just after that, Mr Longnose appeared. This morning, I had a vision that Ms Tulip would give him a riding lesson in the arena and she did. I... I think I might have seer magic – magic that lets me look into the future!"

Moonbeam looked so hopeful that Zara didn't want to disappoint her, but it didn't sound very likely. "Moonbeam, if this was your magic, there should be sparks and you should be able to smell burnt sugar, shouldn't you? That's what happens when the other unicorns use their powers."

"My magic's different," said Moonbeam. "I feel it inside me. It's like having sparks in my head."

"That doesn't sound like magic to me," said

Zara doubtfully.

Moonbeam stamped a hoof in frustration. "So why do I keep seeing the same pictures over and over again? A cloaked man who makes me feel scared, a desert, a damaged green book and rocks falling." She glanced at Zara. "How do you explain that?"

Zara hesitated. "I… I don't know but I'm sure there *is* a logical explanation and I don't think it's because it's your magic." Moonbeam's face fell. Zara felt bad. She hated upsetting her, but she knew it was wrong to lie to her unicorn. "I love you, Moonbeam," she went on awkwardly. "You know that. You're a dreamer and I'm scientific so there are bound to be things we disagree on but just because we're different and don't always agree, it doesn't mean that we can't be really good partners and best friends."

"I guess," sighed Moonbeam. She gave her an anxious look. "But, Zara, promise me you'll be careful when you're spying on Mr Longnose. If he is the cloaked figure I've been seeing in my visions then I don't trust him at all."

Zara hugged her. "That's something we definitely do agree on!" she said with a smile.

CHAPTER FIVE

Zara waited until she and her friends were all back in the dorm and ready for bed before calling a meeting. She told them how she'd followed Mr Longnose to the tower room and how he had vanished into thin air.

Phoebe's eyes widened. "Maybe Mr Longnose can use magic to disappear?"

Zara frowned. "But how? He hasn't got a unicorn and I don't think there's any other magic that can make you vanish. We must keep spying!"

The following day at lunch, Ms Nettles announced

that afternoon lessons were cancelled so that the staff could hold an important meeting.

"Let's go and sneak into Mr Longnose's room while the meeting is going on," said Zara.

The others agreed. They waited until all the adults had gathered together and then they hurried to his room. They tried the door but it was locked.

Zara groaned in frustration. She felt sure if she could search Mr Longnose's room she would find a clue that would prove he was the culprit responsible for the bad weather.

"Never mind," said Lily. "It's boiling inside. Let's make the most of having no lessons and take the unicorns to the meadow. We can all paddle in the stream."

"Not that there's much stream left." Aisha sighed. "I really hope this heatwave doesn't go on much longer. All the streams and rivers are

starting to dry up."

They exchanged anxious looks. The water from Lake Sparkle was magical. Unicorns needed to drink the water in order for their magic to stay strong. It flowed away from the lake around the island in rivers and streams where it nourished crops, people and animals. If the water dried up then the unicorns would lose their magic powers and all of Unicorn Island would suffer.

The girls headed to the stables.

"I've had another vision!" Moonbeam told Zara excitedly when Zara entered her stall. "It happened just now. I saw a dark tunnel. It felt dangerous."

Zara patted her. "OK, well, we'll watch out for dangerous dark tunnels and avoid them," she said, trying, but failing, to hide her grin.

Moonbeam stamped a front hoof. "Don't laugh at me! I'm not making these things up, Zara!"

"Sorry!" Zara said. But it was clear Moonbeam felt hurt. She refused to join Zara in the stream when everyone paddled, even when the paddling ended in a huge water fight. Zara tried being extra nice to her but nothing she said could tempt Moonbeam to join them in the water.

As the sun started to sink in the sky, they headed back to the stables to get the unicorns some sky berries before going in for their own dinner. Sky berries were the unicorns' favourite food. They were full of the vitamins they needed to stay healthy and keep their magic strong. As they passed the barn next to the stables, Zara noticed the big doors were ajar. Hearing a noise, she peeked in and gasped as she saw a tall, thin figure duck behind some hay bales at the far end.

"Come on, Zara, I'm starving!" called Aisha.

Putting her finger to her lips, Zara frantically beckoned her friends over. She pointed to the

bales of hay. "Someone's there," she mouthed. "I think it's Mr Longnose!"

She heard a rustle behind the bales and a soft click.

Zara ran up to the wall of bales. "Got you!" she shouted. She stopped in astonishment as she looked over the top of them. "There's no one here!" she exclaimed.

Phoebe burst out laughing. "You're seeing things, Zara."

"I'm not!" she exclaimed. "I'm sure I saw Mr Longnose!" She saw her friends swapping disbelieving looks.

Zara flushed, suddenly realising how Moonbeam must feel when she wasn't believed. "There *was* someone here."

"OK, but where?" Lily joined her and searched the barn. Suddenly she gasped and pointed to the floor. "What's that?" Crouching down, she

showed Zara a sturdy ring in the floor that had been hidden under the loose hay.

Zara brushed the hay away with her hands. The others, realising they'd found something, crowded round.

"It's the handle of a trap door!" Zara heaved it open and it fell back with a heavy thud.

"It's a secret passage," breathed Phoebe.

"Oh, wow! My mum told me the school has lots of secret passages and tunnels," said Lily. "She and her friends found some when they were here. Maybe this is one of them."

"Let's investigate," said Zara eagerly. "The person I saw just now must have escaped down it. Let's find out where it goes."

"Zara, wait!" Moonbeam stepped forward. "I'm sure this is the dark, dangerous tunnel from my vision."

"Vision?" echoed Phoebe, looking at

Moonbeam. "What are you talking about?"

"It's nothing," Zara said quickly. She didn't want her friends and their unicorns all laughing at Moonbeam. "Just Moonbeam daydreaming as usual. You know what she's like!" She saw a hurt expression cross Moonbeam's face and felt bad, but she was sure that if Moonbeam said she could see into the future everyone would tease her.

"Come on," Zara urged. "Let's see where this goes." She looked round encouragingly at her friends then stepped down into the darkness.

CHAPTER SIX

Phoebe, Lily and Aisha followed Zara into the tunnel. Zara was good at climbing and guided the others, carefully feeling for handholds and footholds in the cold stone wall.

"Be careful!" whinnied the unicorns anxiously as they waited at the top.

"Very, very careful," added Moonbeam.

Once all the girls had climbed down, they set off. Zara traced her hand along the rough stone wall as she edged forward, her eyes gradually getting used to the darkness. She could hear the steady drip of water.

"Eeek!" squealed Phoebe, slipping on a stone.

"Sssh!" Zara stopped, motioning for everyone to be quiet. What if Mr Longnose was ahead of them and heard Phoebe? What if he came back and attacked?

They waited tensely but there was no sound. Cautiously they set off again. The sound of water began to get louder as they walked, until suddenly the tunnel opened into a chamber. Multicoloured water trickled down the damp walls.

"I think we might be under Sparkle Lake."
Zara squinted into the darkness and saw two
more tunnels leading out of the chamber. "There
are two ways out of here—" She gasped as she
spotted something white lying on the floor at
the entrance to one of the tunnels. "Look!" She
hurried to pick it up. It was a white handkerchief
and she could just make out the initials EL in one
corner.

"This belongs to Mr Longnose!" she exclaimed.

"I saw him with it yesterday. He must have dropped it. It's proof he's been down here. He *was* the person I saw come into the tunnel."

Phoebe clutched hold of her. "What should we do?"

Zara took a breath. What if Moonbeam really was having visions and her strange feelings were true? She'd said the tunnel was dangerous. But how could they give up now? They couldn't.

"Let's go on!" she said. The others nodded eagerly.

As Zara walked into the tunnel where the hanky had been lying, she was grateful that her friends were right behind her. The passageway began to climb upwards, getting steeper and narrower until it ended in a small space with a chimney rising up from it. Zara felt around the stones and her hand snagged against something round. Instinctively, she pressed it. There was a grating noise and a

small door swung open.

Ducking through, Zara saw that the door led out into a fireplace in a round room.

"We're in one of the towers in the academy," she said, climbing out.

The others followed her.

"It's a secret room!" Aisha gasped, looking around.

There was an old wooden desk to one side and the walls were lined with curved shelves stacked with glass jars. Over the fireplace hung a portrait of a beautiful unicorn with a long golden mane.

"I wonder what that thing does," said Zara, spotting a lever in the opposite wall and hurrying over. She pulled it and jumped back as the wall started to spin slowly like a revolving door. "This must be the way out!" she said in excitement. The wall revolved back into place. Zara pulled the lever again and this time she and the others

slipped out as the wall turned. They found themselves in a cupboard full of empty cardboard boxes and wooden crates.

"Maybe it's not the way out after all," said Aisha in surprise.

"Wait…" Zara looked around. "This looks familiar. I think it's the cupboard on the landing above Diamond dorm." She spotted the door and turned the handle. It swung open and she stepped out on to the landing between Diamond dorm and the top floor of the tower.

"This is where I lost Mr Longnose yesterday,"

she said excitedly. "So that's why he keeps disappearing. He's using secret tunnels to move around the school!"

"Do you think he heard us following him?" said Phoebe.

"What do you think he will do if he did?" asked Lily.

"Nothing," said Zara, sounding more confident that she felt. "I bet Mr Longnose wouldn't want Ms Nettles to know we found him sneaking around using the secret tunnels, so he won't do anything."

"Shouldn't we tell Ms Nettles?" said Aisha.

Zara thought for a moment. "No. Sneaking around is weird and suspicious but we need proof that he's actually up to no good. We're on to him now. As soon as we find evidence, then we'll tell Ms Nettles. Let's all be careful though, right?"

"Definitely!" said Phoebe. She gave a dramatic

shiver. "After all, we don't know what he's capable of!"

They hurried back to the barn to tell their unicorns what had happened.

"I told you I saw a dangerous tunnel!" Moonbeam muttered to Zara as they walked back to the stable block. "What if Mr Longnose had attacked you? You shouldn't have gone down there."

Zara glanced at her. Moonbeam had been in a bad mood with her ever since she had returned. "We had to. If we hadn't gone down there we wouldn't have found out that Mr Longnose was using the tunnels to sneak around. And it wasn't that dangerous down there. Your feeling was wrong."

"I don't think it was," said Moonbeam tightly. "It could have been dangerous." She gave Zara a reproachful look. "You embarrassed me in front

of everyone back there in the barn, Zara, by saying I'm just daydreaming. I'm not. I'm having *magical visions*. You might not believe it but I know it's true."

She tossed her mane and stomped into her stable. Zara sighed. She wished Moonbeam would stop going on about being able to see into the future. It just wasn't possible! She fetched Moonbeam a big bucket of sky berries but Moonbeam stood at the back of her stable, refusing to look at her.

The girls went to their dorm to wash their hands before dinner. Entering the dining hall, Zara saw Mr Longnose staring at them. His frown left her certain that he'd seen her in the doorway to the barn and knew they had followed him. Zara's appetite left her, even though it was her favourite meal of lasagne followed by ice cream.

After dinner, Ms Nettles clapped her hands for

silence. "The heatwave has gone on much longer than we anticipated. Across the island our rivers and streams are drying up. Mr Longnose has suggested that investigating one of the nearby rivers that is worst hit by the drought might shed some light on the matter. I agree that it will be a useful educational experience and so the whole school will be going on a field trip tomorrow. You can collect your camping equipment and supplies from the hall straight after breakfast. A member of staff will be in charge of each dorm and will show you which part of the river to study." Peering down her nose at the students, Ms Nettles quelled the burst of excited chatter with a stern look. "The groups are Ms Rivers – Opal dorm; Ms Rosemary – Topaz dorm; Ms Tulip and Mr Longnose – Amethyst dorm…"

No! Not him. Zara couldn't believe their bad luck. They were being sent away from the safety of the

academy to a lonely riverside with Mr Longnose! *Ms Tulip will be with us too,* Zara reminded herself. Surely she would protect them if he tried to harm them? *Unless he does something to harm Ms Tulip,* she thought with a shiver.

She looked across at Mr Longnose and saw he was watching them.

Zara felt as if an ice cube was running down her spine. What if Moonbeam actually could see into the future? And what if Mr Longnose was the mysterious, scary cloaked figure Moonbeam had been seeing? They could all be in serious danger!

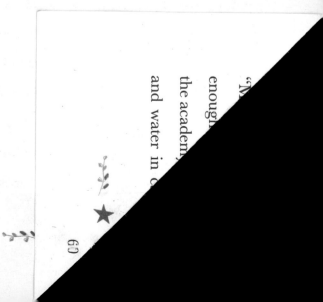

CHAPTER SEVEN

The following morning, Zara, Phoebe, Aisha and Lily went straight to the hall.

"Here are our things," said Lily, seeing a pile of tents, rolled sleeping bags and rucksacks. "How come we seem to have more than everyone else?"

"That's because your dormitory will be going twice as far as everyone else." Mr Longnose came up behind them, making them all jump. "Ms Nettles seems to think you are trustworthy ... to be the group that goes furthest from ... . I insisted that we take sufficient food ... ase we get stuck there for some

reason."

His words had a sinister ring. Goosebumps ran down Zara's arms but she made herself give him a cool look. She was with her friends, their unicorns and Ms Tulip. They were more than a match for him!

She turned her back on Mr Longnose. "Are you ready, Phoebs? Give me a hand with our tent."

"How long do you think we'll have to ride for in order to get to our bit of the river?" said Phoebe.

"No time at all," Mr Longnose smiled thinly. "Ms Nettles has agreed that our group may use the magical map so that we do not waste time travelling."

"The map! Awesome!" breathed Phoebe.

The magical map was a perfect model of Unicorn Island. It stood in the centre of the hall and could take you anywhere on the island. All you had to do was touch your hand to where you

wanted to go and the map would transport you there. Students were only allowed to use it with permission.

"Go and get your unicorns, then meet me and Ms Tulip beside the map," Mr Longnose instructed.

They raced to the stables to collect their unicorns. Moonbeam hardly said a word as they rode back to the school. She was obviously still upset from the previous day. Zara hated the fact they had fallen out. She hoped being on the camping trip would change things.

At last the girls and their unicorns assembled in the hall, weighed down by their camping gear. All the other students and teachers had left for their part of the river. There was just Ms Tulip and Mr Longnose waiting by the map. Ms Tulip was on her unicorn, Rocket, and Mr Longnose was sitting behind her, clutching her tightly.

"I think Mr Longnose still needs some more riding lessons," whispered Lily with a grin.

Zara giggled. Mr Longnose did look very wobbly.

"Toes up!" said Ms Tulip sternly, pointing to his feet.

Zara hid her grin.

"Gather round and hold hands, everyone," said Ms Tulip, riding Rocket closer to the map

"Isn't it beautiful?" whispered Phoebe, gazing at the miniature island.

"It is," answered Zara as she took her hand. "But look at how much damage the heatwave has caused." Tiny palm trees waved in patches along the coastline but the rest of the island looked parched and the streams and rivers had nearly disappeared.

"Ready for the Rushing River?" Ms Tulip touched a long thin river that snaked through the

dry landscape.

Zara gasped as the world started to spin and a wind blew up around them. Suddenly they were turning and tumbling through the air.

Moonbeam's hooves touched solid ground and Zara blinked in the bright sunlight.

They were standing on the bank of an exposed riverbed that was cracked and dusty. A thin stream of water flowed slowly down the middle of what should have been a wide, fast river. Zara looked round and saw all her friends and their unicorns had arrived safely. Mr Longnose was hanging on to Rocket's side, his face pale. Looking embarrassed, he hastily sat up and straightened his tie.

Ms Tulip opened up her hand to reveal a small model of the academy. "This will allow us to return to the academy whenever we want," she said with a smile. "I'll put it in my tent to keep it safe until we have finished our studies."

A little way beyond the riverbed was a small copse of dry, spindly trees. The unicorns trotted over to it to shelter from the sun with Moonbeam trailing dreamily behind. The girls and teachers

pitched their tents next to them.

Mr Longnose called for everyone to gather round. "We need to start collecting soil samples from the riverbed. Each sample you take should be put into a test tube and labelled with its exact location. You may work in pairs. Now, off you go!"

They collected their equipment from Ms Tulip and walked along the dried-up riverbed. The work wasn't hard but it was repetitive and the sun bore down on them from a cloudless sky. By midday, everyone was hot, sticky and tired.

"Lunch!" called Ms Tulip, appearing from her tent with flasks of cold fruit juice.

"Thank goodness." Phoebe flapped her sun hat in front of her face to cool herself down. "I think I'm going to die of thirst."

While they ate their lunch, Ms Tulip chattered to the girls while Mr Longnose sat slightly off to one side.

"I'm looking forward to this evening when it'll be cooler," Aisha said to Ms Tulip. "Can we light a fire and toast marshmallows?"

Mr Longnose sniffed with disapproval. "You will not. It's far too dangerous to start a fire in these conditions."

"This trip isn't going to be any fun at all," Phoebe grumbled quietly to Zara.

"I think I'll take a walk before we get started again. Does anyone want to join me?" said Ms Tulip.

"I'll come." Mr Longnose was on his feet in an instant.

"Anyone else?" Ms Tulip asked, and Mr Longnose looked relieved when everyone shook their heads.

"We won't be long," Ms Tulip said as the pair set off.

Zara watched them walk along the riverbank

and once they were out of sight, she jumped up. "This is our chance to investigate Mr Longnose! Someone keep a lookout while I search his tent!"

CHAPTER EIGHT

"Is this a good idea?" Lily asked anxiously as Zara ran to Mr Longnose's tent and lifted the entrance flap. "What if he catches us?"

"I'll watch out and if he comes back unexpectedly then I'll pretend to have heatstroke!" said Phoebe.

"I'll help Zara search. Lily, you keep a lookout with Phoebe," said Aisha.

Zara ducked into Mr Longnose's tent. It was very neat and tidy. A pair of checked pyjamas was folded neatly on top of his sleeping bag.

"These are identical to my grandad's," giggled

Aisha. "He's got a teddy bear!" she added, snorting with laughter. She held up a small bear covered with pink love hearts. "Look at this!"

"Hang on. I've found something!" Zara held up a slim green exercise book from Mr Longnose's rucksack. The book triggered a memory. Someone had mentioned a green book recently, but who was it? She opened it. It was filled with notes and diagrams. She squeaked as she read a heading: *How to Cause Purple Tornadoes*.

Heart racing, she carried the book outside. Why did Mr Longnose have a book with notes on

how to cause purple tornadoes? There was only one possible explanation!

Moonbeam whinnied in surprise. "Zara! I know that book! I've seen it in my visions. Was it in Mr Longnose's tent?"

"Yes," said Zara. "Are you sure it's the one you saw in your vision though?"

Moonbeam nodded hard. "Open it and you'll find a brown ring on the inside cover that looks like it was made by a cup."

Zara turned the book in her hands. The cover page was ripped and it was impossible to read the title. Opening it up, she saw a faded brown stain the same size as the base of a cup just as Moonbeam had described. She caught her breath. How was that possible?

"I told you I saw it," said Moonbeam softly, nudging her with her nose.

"Wow! You really saw it in a vision? That's

amazing, Moonbeam!" said Phoebe.

Moonbeam nodded. "I … I think I might be a seer. It's a rare kind of magic that allows glimpses of the future."

"You've found your magic?" said Lily in delight. "I can't believe you didn't tell us!"

Moonbeam looked uncertain. "I don't know for sure yet. Zara doesn't think it is."

Zara bit her lip as her friends all gave her surprised looks. "We'll talk about this later," she said quickly. Hurt flashed across Moonbeam's eyes. "I'm sorry, Moonbeam, but for now we need to focus on this book. It's real evidence that Mr Longnose is involved with all the environmental disasters." She held it up. "It's got notes on how to cause a purple tornado and also –" she flicked the pages over – "how to cause a volcano to erupt and how to direct a tidal wave. This is the proof we need!"

"I knew it!" cried Phoebe. "Now we can tell everyone what an evil villain he is!"

"Are you sure it is Mr Longnose's writing?" Aisha asked.

"I don't know," said Zara, suddenly realising she hadn't thought about that.

"It's got to be his book if it was in his tent," argued Lily.

"It seems likely but Aisha's right – how do we know for sure he made these notes?" admitted Zara. She leafed through a few more pages. "Hey, have any of you heard of sun pearls?" she said, seeing a page entitled: *How to cause a drought with sun pearls.* They shook their heads.

Zara's eyes skimmed the page. "It says here that while rain seeds can be used to make it rain, sun pearls can be used to cause a drought."

She read the notes out loud: "*Once the sun pearls are safely hidden in a place where the sun will shine on*

them all day, the drought spreads rapidly. The spell can only be reversed by finding the sun pearls, putting them in a dried-up water source and asking a unicorn to shed a tear on them." She turned the page over but it was blank. "Maybe Mr Longnose is using sun pearls to cause this drought!"

"And if we find the sun pearls he's used, we can stop it!" said Lily in excitement.

"But how do we find them?" said Aisha. "They could be anywhere!"

Moonbeam stepped forward. "Maybe my magic can help?" she said shyly. "I could try to have a vision about them – it might give us some clue as to where they are."

"Go on – try!" urged Phoebe.

"I don't know if it will work," warned Moonbeam. "Visions usually just come to me, I've never tried to have one on demand. But I'll have a go."

Zara burned with embarrassment as Moonbeam took a few steps away from them and closed her eyes. If this failed, Moonbeam was going to look so silly. Lily squeezed her arm. "It's OK," she whispered. "Even if it doesn't work, it's worth trying. Go and tell Moonbeam you believe in her. It'll make her magic stronger."

Zara reminded herself about the stain inside the book. There was no way Moonbeam could have known about that unless her visions were real. *Maybe she's right and I'm wrong,* she thought.

She walked over to Moonbeam and put her arms around her neck. "You can do this, Moonbeam," she said. "You *can* see into the future. I believe you." Moonbeam gave her a grateful look and then shut her eyes.

For a moment nothing happened but then she started to sway slightly. "I see a barren red desert," she said dreamily. "And there's a rock that looks

like a bear. There's something on its nose. A shiny silver disc with some tiny white beads suspended above it. They're burning hot."

"Sun pearls, I bet!" breathed Phoebe.

Moonbeam's voice rose. "I see a cloaked man now. He is angry. The earth … the earth is shaking. Rocks are falling from the sky. Zara!" Moonbeam's eyes snapped open. Her nostrils flared and she was trembling. She stared at Zara with wide eyes. "I saw you in danger," she breathed.

Zara felt a shiver run through her but she forced

herself to stay calm. So what if Moonbeam had seen her in danger? From what she had said, it sounded like they all might be in danger! "Tell me about the man you saw," she said. "Was it Mr Longnose?"

"He was turned away from me so I couldn't see his face," said Moonbeam. "He was tall and thin."

"Like Mr Longnose," gasped Phoebe.

"We need to find the place Moonbeam saw," said Lily. "And get those sun pearls."

"If it had red soil, it might be the Ember Sands," said Zara. "There's a huge rock there called the Bear. It's incredibly remote and very hot. It would be the perfect place to hide sun pearls."

"Should we tell Ms Tulip?" said Aisha.

"Definitely," said Lily.

"No! Wait!" Phoebe said urgently. "I really like Ms Tulip but, think about it, she's been spending

a lot of time with Mr Longnose recently. What if she's now in league with him?"

"Ms Tulip? No way, she'd never harm the island," said Aisha. "She's much too nice."

"But what if the niceness is just an act!" exclaimed Phoebe. "What if she's in Mr Longnose's thrall?" She shook her head. "We can't risk it. I think we should use the model to go back to school and show Ms Nettles the book."

Zara's mind raced. Like Aisha, she found it almost impossible to believe that Ms Tulip might have turned evil, but could they risk it? No. "You're right, Phoebs," she decided. "Let's go now before Ms Tulip and Mr Longnose get back."

She ducked into Ms Tulip's tent and took the model of the academy from the teacher's bag. The girls mounted their unicorns and linked hands. "Unicorn Academy!" they cried together.

The wind whipped up and they found

themselves spinning round until their unicorns' hooves hit hard ground. Opening their eyes, they realised they were back in the hall of the academy.

"Let's find Ms Nettles!" cried Zara.

The girls raced to Ms Nettles' office. The door was open and her desk was neat and tidy, but there was no sign of her. They tried her bedroom and the stables but the academy was as empty as a ghost school. They ran back to the hall.

"Where is Ms Nettles?" said Lily in frustration.

Zara glanced out through the large windows, taking in the scorched grass and the shrinking lake. "I don't know, but we're running out of time. We've got to try and fix the drought ourselves. Let's use the map to go to the Ember Sands, find the sun pearls and end the heatwave. Then we can come back and find Ms Nettles."

"But, Zara!" protested Moonbeam. "In my vision, I saw you in danger in the desert. I saw the earth shaking and rocks raining down from the sky."

"It doesn't rain rocks, silly," said Zara. "That bit of your vision must have been wrong. I'll be fine." She went over and stroked Moonbeam's nose. "Moonbeam, we have to stop the drought before it's too late! Please say you'll come with me."

"Of course I'll come!" said Moonbeam.

"There's no way I'll let you face danger alone."

Zara beamed. Despite their differences, she and Moonbeam were partners and they were there for each other when it mattered. "Thanks," she whispered, kissing her. Remembering that Moonbeam had said about the sun pearls being burning hot, she ran over to the fireplace and pocketed the fireproof gloves hanging there. Then she vaulted on to her back. "Come on, everyone! It's time to travel to the Ember Sands!"

CHAPTER NINE

They all held hands and Zara touched the map. A warm wind carried the girls and their unicorns to the Ember Sands. The dusty red ground was parched and the desert seemed to stretch on for miles with nothing but thorny bushes and giant balls of springy tumbleweed to break up the monotony. The magic set the group down beside a huge rock. It towered over them and they stepped gratefully into its shade.

Zara gazed up. The great mass of red rock looked just like a lumbering grizzly bear. *Bear rock!* Zara gasped. Moonbeam had said that the

sun pearls were on the bear's nose, but it was impossible to see from down here. There was only one way to find out if they were actually there.

"I'll climb up to the nose," she said to the others. "It shouldn't be too bad. There are plenty of handholds and footholds."

"But—" Moonbeam began.

"No, Moonbeam, it should be me. I'm the best at climbing."

"I'll come with you," said Aisha.

"I'll find it easier to concentrate on my own," said Zara. She didn't want to have to worry about someone else being in danger. She studied the rock for a moment and then began to pull herself up its craggy face. She was a good climber but she had never climbed so high before. She went up and up, stopping occasionally to work out the best place for her sweaty hands to find a grip. Her friends' voices drifted up to her, shouting

encouragement.

Zara finally reached the bear's head and stopped to catch her breath. Glancing down, her stomach lurched. The ground was so far away and her friends looked so small! To her surprise, she realised that Moonbeam wasn't watching her. She was talking to Feather, who was stamping her hooves, sending pink sparks into the air. Whatever were they doing?

Zara frowned and tore her eyes away. She couldn't afford to be distracted. Somehow, she had to edge up on to the head and then climb out on to the long protrusion of rock that formed the bear's nose. She could see a strange silver disc balanced on it, like an enormous shiny saucer. A pillar in the centre of the disc was holding up a collection of round white objects. Sun pearls! She was sure of it! Her heart lifted. Moonbeam's vision had been right. *I'll give her a huge hug when*

I get down and tell her I'm sorry I ever doubted her, she thought.

She pulled herself up the bear's head and, with her feet balancing on the narrow footholds, crept across the face towards the nose. She swung herself up, her legs straddling it as if she were riding a unicorn. The sun pearls were shining brightly, their magic coming to life in the rays of the fierce desert sun. Zara realised that the shiny surface of the disc must be reflecting the heat back on to the pearls, amplifying their magic and sending it all over the island. She could feel heat radiating from them. She would have to edge along the rock until she could reach the burning pearls. She just hoped the nose would hold her weight as well as the weight of the disc.

She slowly crept towards the pearls. She pulled on one of the fireproof gloves then, bending forward and hanging on to the nose with one arm, she stretched her gloved hand out, but she couldn't quite reach them over the edge of the disc. She wriggled further, straining until – finally! – her fingers touched the pearls. Suddenly, the rock began to shake. She heard her friends cry out and the unicorns whinny in alarm. It was an earth tremor!

Forgetting about the pearls, Zara pulled her hand back and hung on to the rock for dear life, clinging like a limpet to the bear's nose as the world shook violently. The tremor lasted a minute and then stopped.

Zara and Moonbeam

"Zara! Are you OK?" Moonbeam whinnied.

"Yes!" Zara shouted, although every cell in her body felt like it was trembling. "I've reached the pearls now. I'll be down soon. Don't worry!"

She leaned forward and, this time, her hand closed around the shining spheres. Just at that moment there was another tremor and the rock started to shake violently. Zara was only holding on with one hand and it wasn't enough. She felt herself slip and scrabbled for a handhold but with a yell she began to fall!

She rushed towards the ground, her arms flailing. She waited to hit the hard earth but instead she landed on a huge mound of springy tumbleweed. She bounced up into the air with a surprised shriek. It was like being on a giant trampoline. How had it got there to break her fall?

As she slowly came to rest, she heard the

clamour of her friends' voices and the unicorns' whinnies. She sat up, her hair sticking out wildly. "What just happened?" she gasped, her heart pounding.

Moonbeam cantered over. "I knew you were going to fall. I saw it in a vision as you were climbing up so I asked Feather to use her magic to pull the tumbleweed into place just before the earth tremor so it would soften your landing."

Zara stared. "Moonbeam! Oh, wow!" Shoving the pearls and glove in her pocket, she slid off the giant cushion of tumbleweed and flung her arms

around Moonbeam's neck. "Thank you so much! You saved my life!"

There was another rumble and the ground shook even more strongly. "I haven't finished saving it yet!" whinnied Moonbeam in alarm as there was a loud creaking sound from above them. "On my back! NOW!" Zara didn't stop to ask why. Trusting Moonbeam, she scrambled on her back. Just as they leapt away there was an enormous cracking sound and the bear's nose broke into pieces. Rocks rained down, crashing into the ground where seconds before Moonbeam and Zara had been standing.

Moonbeam skidded to a halt by the others.

"Oh, my goodness, are you both OK?" Phoebe's eyes were wide with shock.

"Yes, thanks to Moonbeam," stammered Zara, her heart pounding like a drum. "I'll never doubt your magic again, Moonbeam. I promise!"

"No way! Look at that!" shrieked Phoebe, pointing over Zara's shoulder. "Someone's seriously out to get us!"

Zara looked round and saw a whirling red sandstorm sweeping towards them, its sharp grains swirling viciously.

"Leave this one to me!" whinnied Shimmer.

He stamped his front hooves. Sparks flew up and the sweet smell of burning sugar tingled in their nostrils. The ground seemed to ripple as a wave of energy swept from Shimmer towards the sandstorm. As it reached it, the sandstorm exploded, red sand shooting up into the air.

A man's voice boomed out across the desert. "You children cannot stop me! Soon everyone on this island will realise that I can do far more than unicorns can do on their own!" His cackling laughter bounced around the rock, sending chills shivering along Zara's spine.

"We need to leave right now!" she shouted. "Moonbeam is right! This place is full of danger. The sand pearls must have been protected by dark spells which were triggered when I took the pearls! Come on!" She pulled the model of the school out of her pocket. The others grabbed each other's hands.

The next moment, they felt themselves being swept up in a cloud of sparkles and whisked away.

CHAPTER TEN

The magic set them down safely back in the hall of the academy. For a moment, they all stood there, catching their breath.

"That was the scariest thing EVER!" said Phoebe shakily.

For once, Zara didn't tease her for being overly dramatic. "It really was. Oh, Moonbeam!" She leaned forward and flung her arms round Moonbeam's neck as she buried her face in her long silver mane. "Thank you so much for saving me – twice. Seer magic is awesome."

Moonbeam turned her head to nuzzle her. "I

didn't see everything. My magic only gave me glimpses. I saw visions of you and the rocks falling. I heard a man's evil laughter and I worked out what was going to happen." Moonbeam smiled shyly at Zara. "I used the evidence. I could see that the bear's nose didn't look very stable. When the tremors started, I guessed that you would fall and the rocks would come crashing down on you so I worked out how to keep you safe. I'm not going to rely just on predictions in the future, I'll use evidence too."

Zara grinned. "And I'm definitely not going to rely just on evidence, I'm going to listen to your feelings. If it hadn't been for your magic, Moonbeam, we wouldn't have found the sun pearls. I wish I'd listened to you sooner."

Phoebe gasped and pointed. "Your hair! Zara! You've got a silver streak — the same colour as Moonbeam's mane. You've bonded!"

Zara swept her fingers through her hair, searching for the coloured streak. She gasped. Phoebe was right!

The other unicorns whinnied and the girls cheered.

"You've bonded! You've bonded!" sung Aisha.

Zara beamed. She and Moonbeam were partners for life now and would be able to graduate together at the end of the year.

"Let's go and break the sun pearls' spell!" Moonbeam whinnied. "We can use Sparkle Lake."

They cantered out of the school hall and raced to the lake. The water was shrinking fast. The lake was much smaller than it usually was.

"Ready to break the drought?" Zara called.

"Ready!" her friends yelled back.

They walked on to the solid mud surrounding the lake and stood in a circle. Zara pulled out the sun pearls and placed them on the mud in a little pile. They glittered brightly in the sunshine. "Unicorns, it's your turn," said Zara. "We need one of you to cry."

"I'll do it," Moonbeam said softly. She smiled at Zara and a happy tear rolled down her cheek. "I'm just so glad that you believe in me now and we've bonded." She let her tear fall on the pyramid of sun pearls.

Zara and Moonbeam

The sun pearls hissed as her tear fell on them and they began to glow a blueish-green. A fresh wind blew up and grey rain clouds scudded across the sky. The sun disappeared behind the clouds and for once none of the girls minded.

We did it!" Zara jumped up and down in joy as the rain fell, soaking everyone and sinking into the parched ground. The girls ran to the banks and spun round, letting the rain splash on to their faces as all around them the dry grass began to turn

back to green and the wilting flowers came to life again, the flower heads bursting into bloom.

Soaked but happy, the girls rode through the rain to the stable block. Just as they reached it, Ms Nettles came cantering towards them on her unicorn, Thyme.

"Amethyst dorm! Whatever are you doing back?" she said in concern. "Where are Ms Tulip and Mr Longnose?"

"We were looking for you, Ms Nettles, but you weren't here," said Zara, ignoring her questions.

"I was at an urgent meeting with the school governors to discuss the extreme weather, but the measures we put in place are no longer needed," said Ms Nettles. "Can you believe it, girls?" Her face broke into a smile, very different from her usual strict expression. "I never thought I'd be so happy to see rain!"

"We made it happen!" Phoebe said.

Ms Nettles blinked. "You did? How?"

They all explained.

"It's got to be Mr Longnose who's to blame for everything!" Zara finished. "You have to do something about him, Ms Nettles."

"Have you got the notebook?" Ms Nettles said quickly.

Zara handed it over. Ms Nettles opened it. "But this isn't Mr Longnose's handwriting," she said. She looked inside the front page. "And look, here are some initials," she pointed to some faded letters. "L.T. Not E.L, which are Mr Longnose's initials. He may have had the book in his tent, but it doesn't look like it belongs to him."

"He could still have used it even if he didn't write it!" argued Zara.

"We're sure it's him, Ms Nettles!" said Lily.

"Girls, what you are accusing Mr Longnose of is a very serious crime," said Ms Nettles.

99

"We cannot make accusations without sufficient evidence."

"You know something?" said Aisha suddenly. "I'm not sure it is Mr Longnose."

They turned to look at her in surprise.

"The voice in the sandstorm – I heard it clearly this time and it wasn't Mr Longnose's voice," said Aisha. "It was different."

"You're right," said Phoebe, frowning. She imitated the deep voice. "*You cannot stop me!*"

Zara frowned. If the voice in the sandstorm wasn't Mr Longnose's then maybe he wasn't responsible for all the weather disasters after all. But why was Mr Longnose acting so suspiciously – unless he was helping the real villain?

"Leave this now, girls," Ms Nettles instructed. "I shall look into it, but while I do, I must ask you to keep your suspicions to yourselves. Will you do that?"

They nodded.

"Good. Now, I must use the map to go to the Rushing River and explain to Ms Tulip and Mr Longnose where you all are. They're going to

10

be frantic with worry." Ms Nettles straightened her glasses. "And while we are unsure about Mr Longnose, I'll make up an excuse for you having left so suddenly – I'll say Moonbeam discovered her magic and you wanted to come and tell me about a vision she'd had.

"I really am grateful to you for breaking the drought. Your actions and bravery have saved the island and our dear academy. Now, it's hardly weather for camping," she said, gesturing at the rain, "but how would you like a special sleepover in the stables? I'll ask the kitchens to send you a picnic."

The girls grinned at each other. "Totally awesome!" said Phoebe. "You're the best, Ms Nettles!"

Looking pleased, Ms Nettles rode off towards the hall.

The girls fed the unicorns massive buckets of

sky berries and dried them off. By the time they had finished, the kitchen staff had laid out a huge picnic blanket covered with sandwiches, crisps and cakes. Feather used her magic to bring the camping gear they needed from the hall. The girls laid their cosy sleeping bags around the blanket and settled down to their feast.

After they had eaten, Zara jumped to her feet. "Who's up for a game of tag?"

"Me!" everyone shouted.

"You can be *it*, Zara!" said Phoebe. "Hide, everyone, before they tag us!" Phoebe vaulted on Shimmer and they galloped away to hide. The others quickly followed.

"Not fair!" said Zara, looking around at the suddenly empty space.

"Don't worry, I've got this." Moonbeam shut her eyes and swayed from side to side. "I see a girl with black hair and a unicorn with a green, silver

and red mane galloping out from the trees in a few minutes."

"Aisha and Silver!" Zara exclaimed, hugging Moonbeam. "We can go and lie in wait for them." She grinned. "You know, something tells me we might just win this game, Moonbeam!"

"I definitely won when I got paired with you," said Moonbeam, nuzzling her.

Zara's heart swelled with happiness. "I feel exactly the same," she said. "I wouldn't want any other unicorn but you."

Zara vaulted on to Moonbeam's back. "Watch out, everyone! We're coming for you, ready or not!"

She whooped as Moonbeam galloped away, leaving a trail of silvery hoofprints on the glittering, rain-soaked grass.

PRINCESS of PETS

Animal adventures, friendship and a royal family! From the author of The Rescue Princesses.

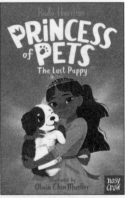

Another MAGICAL series from Nosy Crow!

SNOW SiSTERS